Bima
and the
Water of Life

by

Franzeska G. Ewart

Illustrated by Sandeep Kaushik

To David Powell, with love

First published in 2007 in Great Britain by
Barrington Stoke Ltd
18 Walker St, Edinburgh, EH3 7LP

www.barringtonstoke.co.uk

ISBN: 978-1-84299-509-9

Printed in Great Britain by Bell & Bain Ltd

Contents

WITHDRAWN FROM STOCK

Chapter 1
The Birth of Bima

Bima was the biggest, strongest, and bravest hero in all of India.

He was so strong he could lift mountains. In fact, people said he was as strong as 10,000 elephants! When he stamped his foot the forest shook, and when he walked, his footsteps made the earth quake.

And he was afraid of no one. There was no monster too scary for Bima to fight, and no giant too big for him to kill.

For Bima, you see, was not like other men. He and his four brothers lived with their mother, Queen Khundi, and their father, King Pandu. But King Pandu wasn't Bima's real father. Bima's *real* father was Vayu, the Wind God. And Vayu was magic, and his magic was very powerful ...

He could turn himself into a hurricane and pull trees up by their roots.

He could turn himself into a tornado and make the sea into a huge whirl-pool that sucked everything down.

And he could catch the rain, and the snow, and the hail in his mouth. Then he could spit them out with such a force they could knock a man down.

With a father like that, Bima *had* to be a hero. And what a hero he was! Like his father, he could control the wind, and he loved adventure. No challenge, no matter how great the danger, was too much for him.

Bima looked like a hero, too. He was a huge man! His hair was thick and black. His eyes were balls of orange fire, and he had a black and white snake round his neck. His arms were as thick as tree trunks. He liked to fight with his bare hands, or with a wooden club.

Bima's colossal size, and his huge arms, and his mighty club made everyone shake with fear – but they were nothing compared to the power he held in his thumb-nails!

For, strange as it may sound, Bima, like his father, had magic thumb-nails, and they were his most powerful weapon. Huge, curved, and pointed, like daggers, they could rip his enemies to bits. And he always kept them sharp!

By now you must be thinking that Bima was a very scary man, and of course you'd be right. But, although Bima was a terrible enemy, he was also the kindest, most loving friend anyone could ever ask for. More than anything, he was very, very honest.

Now, even though Bima grew up to be a big, powerful man, he had a difficult start in life. When Bima was a baby, he was trapped inside a stone shell! It covered his little body, and stopped him from growing. And, as he was a baby, he wasn't yet strong enough to break out.

Sometimes he'd cry out in pain and anger. No matter how he tried to struggle out, he was trapped inside his stone prison.

His mother and father were very sad. They knew that Bima should be a great warrior, and it broke their hearts to hear him crying. So they sent for the strongest men in the land, and begged them to help.

From far and wide they came, and, one after the other, they tried to break the shell. Some hit it with their swords. Some hammered it with tree trunks. Some dropped it off high cliffs, but nothing worked. That stone shell just would not crack.

In the end, King Pandu and Queen Khundi sent for one of Bima's cousins, Suyudana. He left his grand palace and came, bringing his army with him.

Hundreds of soldiers on war-horses attacked the stone shell from all sides, but it was no good. They couldn't even chip off a tiny bit!

"It can't be done," Suyudana told Bima's parents. "I'm afraid your Bima will never grow."

The king and queen were heart-broken. It seemed as if no one could help their son. Bima's cries got so loud they upset the forest, and then the Earth, and then the Universe.

At last they grew so loud they were heard by a wise man, a great Guru, who sent help. But did he send an army of strong men? No! He sent an elephant.

It was no ordinary elephant though. Its name was Sena, and it had magic powers.

From every corner of the land, people came to see the mighty Sena try to break the stone shell. Everyone knew this was Bima's last chance of a normal life. If Sena failed, what future did he have?

Again and again the elephant ran at the stone shell, blowing hard through its trunk and crashing down on the shell with its rock-hard feet.

Still the shell would not break.

At last, with one great trumpet-blast, the elephant thrust its magic tusks under Bima's stone prison and threw it high up into the air. Everyone gasped as it spun round and round, and up and up. Then it turned and fell, like a meteor, to the ground. With an ear-splitting CRACK! the shell smashed into a thousand bits, and Bima jumped out.

Everyone was over-joyed! They held a party for many days and nights. No one could have been more happy than the king and queen.

One person, however, was not happy. When Bima's cousin Suyudana heard the news, he could hardly believe his ears.

"An *elephant?*" he shouted. "An elephant is just an animal – how could it have done what I failed to do?"

And he jumped on his horse and galloped like the wind to see for himself.

When he saw that Bima really was free, Suyudana was filled with rage. So great was his anger that people say he turned bright red! The months passed, and Bima grew and grew into a super-human hero. And Suyudana's anger grew too.

Suyudana knew, you see, he'd never win a fight against Bima, for Bima would always be stronger. So Suyudana swore that, one day, he'd kill him.

And this is the story of how he tried ...

Chapter 2
Durna's Quest

One day, Bima went to Suyudana's palace. He wanted to see his old teacher, Durna, who lived and worked there.

"The very person I've been looking for," said Durna with a big smile. "I have a quest for you!"

Bima looked down in surprise at his teacher's bent little body. Long ago, Durna had been in a fight, and his broken nose and twisted left arm showed how badly he'd lost!

"A quest?" Bima repeated, his eyes gleaming like hot coals. Then he drew himself up to his full height and puffed out his big chest.

"Give me any challenge you like, Durna," he thundered. "Nothing is too much for me!"

Durna smiled. He knew his pupil well. Bima was so brave, and so stubborn, that he would do almost anything, whatever the danger.

"I want you to go in search of the secret cave that holds the Water of Life," Durna told him. "That water has magic powers. If you drink it, you will be pure, and very wise."

Without stopping to think, Bima agreed. Then he strode off home, stepping over mountains and forests with the greatest of ease, to tell his family.

But when Bima's mother heard what he planned to do, she was filled with horror.

"The danger will be far too great!" she said.

"And who knows the real reason why Durna's given you this quest," she went on. "He works for Suyudana. Do you think you should trust him?"

Bima listened to all his mother said. Then he went away and thought about it.

She was right, he knew – the quest would be full of danger. But he loved danger! And as for not trusting Durna, his old teacher – how silly that seemed to him. For Bima was an honest man, and honest people sometimes can't believe that others could be *dis*honest.

So, the next day, in spite of his mother's warning, Bima went to tell Durna he would go in search of the Water of Life.

With a great whirl-wind of a roar, Bima rushed off to the palace. As he stormed through the forest, animals ran away. At the thundering of his footsteps, birds flew high into the sky.

When Bima arrived at the palace, he saw that Durna was not alone. By his side stood Suyudana, dressed in his robes and crown.

The moment Suyudana saw Bima, he shook with fear. He had forgotten how big and strong his cousin was. And, as always, he asked himself, *why did that elephant crack open Bima's shell? WHY?*

"So you have come to take up the challenge, Bima," Suyudana said, with a charming smile. "Well done! The Water of

Life will make you pure, and so wise that you will truly understand yourself."

He and Durna gazed up at Bima. Then they smiled at one another.

"Now, brave Bima," said Durna, "listen well, and I will tell you how to find the secret cave which contains that magic water."

Suddenly Bima felt that something was wrong. He had seen the way the two men smiled at one another. Something about that smile made him suspect a trap. He thought back to what his mother had said. Was she right? Should he trust Durna and Suyudana?

"Perhaps ..." he said slowly, "... I don't want to become pure and wise after all ..."

Bima began to back away.

"Wait, Bima!" Durna cried, his voice high with panic. "There's something else that the Water of Life will give you ..."

"Something that we're sure you will want ..." said Suyudana, giving Bima a wink.

Bima stopped in his tracks. "And what is that?" he asked.

Suyudana's dark eyes glinted. "Ever-lasting happiness," he said simply.

"For yourself," Durna added, "and anyone you care to give it to."

Bima thought about it. What could be better than to have happiness all your life, and – even better – be able to give that happiness to everyone you loved?

He looked down at his big, strong club. He rubbed each of his dagger-sharp thumbnails with his sleeve. They looked lethal. All his fears faded away like snow-flakes on a river.

Of *course* he could trust his cousin and his teacher. His mother was just being silly! And as for dangers – of course there would be many, but wasn't he as brave as any hero? Weren't his weapons as strong as anyone else's?

"I'll do it," he said, and he listened as Durna told him the way to the cave. Then, not wanting to waste another moment, he lifted up his club and marched out of the palace.

With huge steps that hit the ground like thunder-bolts, Bima set off towards the mountains, to find the cave that held the Water of Life.

He was sure he was doing the right thing. But, way at the back of his mind, was Suyudana's smiling face and the glint in his dark eyes. And every night, as Bima lay down, the memory of that glint slid, like a deadly snake, into his head.

Had it just been sun-light reflecting off Suyudana's crown? Or did it show that there was evil in his mind?

Chapter 3
The Wicked Ogre

For many days Bima strode on, in search of the secret cave which held the Water of Life.

Each night, the memory of Suyudana's cunning look upset his dreams. But when the sun rose, he pushed the memory away. Then off he went, striding over trees and rivers and mountains, following Durna's directions.

Durna had told him that the cave was hidden deep in the side of a steep mountain, and to reach the mountain he must find his way through a thick forest. Durna had also warned that many dangers hid in the dark of the forest.

And indeed, as Bima strode deeper and deeper into the forest, huge trees stood above him, and blotted out the sun's light. Wild beasts howled and roared from the shadows, and birds screeched warning-calls.

But Bima felt no fear. The thought of the Water of Life gave him all the courage he needed.

One morning, however, Bima heard a sound on the breeze that made him reach for his club. It was a terrible growling, and he knew at once that it didn't come from an animal. Only an ogre – an ugly, wicked monster – could make such an ugly, angry sound. Nothing is more wicked than an ogre.

Holding up his club, Bima crept towards the sound of the growling. Then he pushed the trees to one side as if they were tiny bushes. He knew he had to find and kill the wicked ogre. If he didn't, it would find him. And, as likely as not, it would be hungry and looking for a meal – and what could be more tasty to an ogre than human flesh!

At last Bima was so close he could smell the big brute. It was sniffing, pig-like, along the forest path. With one great leap, and a roar like the North Wind, Bima was on top of it, pinning it down with his great weight.

How the ogre's huge round eyes glared up at him! How its sharp teeth shone, and its hot breath filled his nose with the foul smell of rotting flesh! It pushed against Bima, growling with rage. Its huge hands were

death-white and clammy. And its claws made red gashes in the noble brown skin of Bima's face. But still Bima crouched above it, like a great stone tiger.

The forest stood silent as Bima struggled with the ogre; but at last that struggle was over. Raising himself up on one hand, Bima drew back his mighty arm, and with one swipe of his glinting thumb-nail, slit the monster's throat. Then, taking no notice of the river of blood that gushed from the wound, he cut its head clean off.

How proud he felt as he held it up! He had rid the forest of one of its evil monsters – and what a prize he had to take back to Durna.

Bima lifted the head onto his back and went on his way. Slowly, the forest came back to life. Birds sang and monkeys chattered. Everyone was grateful to their hero. And every song, every squeal, every bark and every howl seemed to wish him well on his quest.

Late that afternoon, as the sun was setting and the shadows were growing long, Bima sat down to rest. Looking ahead through the dark forest, he felt a wave of excitement rise in his belly. For he could see that there were fewer trees now and the ground no longer felt damp and soft, but rocky and dry.

It was just as Durna said – he was nearing the end of the forest. Tomorrow, he would do what he set out to do. Tomorrow, he would find the Water of Life.

Bima settled down to sleep, the ogre's head beside him. But in the morning, when he reached the edge of the forest and climbed up the steep mountain, he couldn't see the cave anywhere.

In a panic Bima searched everywhere. He uprooted high trees and turned over huge rocks, sending them tumbling down into the valley below. At last, hidden deep in the rock face, he found it – the cave that held the Water of Life.

Bima gazed at the cave in wonder. It was huge. It looked like a big gash in the mountain's stony flesh. *But instead of blood*, thought Bima with joy in his heart, *magic water would gush from that wound!*

He stepped nearer, hoping to hear the sound of water, but there was none. Nor was there any wetness on the sides of the cave. Its rocks were grey and dry, and the only sound to echo from inside was a low and distant rumble.

And the rumbling was growing louder, and more ominous, by the second.

Bima's blood ran cold. Now he knew that his mother had been right not to trust Durna and Suyudana. They *had* been up to no good, for they had sent him into a trap.

For sure, this dark, dry cave had no Water of Life inside it ... but what did it hold?

Bima moved closer and listened. The noise echoed from one wall to the other, and the ground shook. Heavy foot-steps thundered up from the cave.

Echoing footsteps ... First one set, then another ...

The day was warm, but Bima shivered. An awful thought had struck him, like a deadly blow from a club.

Could it be that these foot-steps were not echoes? Could it be that there were two pairs of feet?

Now even Bima, with all his strength and courage, began to back away from the mouth of the cave. For suddenly he knew what was inside, and he shook his great head in horror.

Could Suyudana, his cousin, have wished him such a terrible end? Could Durna, his old teacher, really have sent him to meet *this* dreadful fate? How cruel these men had been. Bima, whose heart was always full of kindness, could have wept. He had trusted them, but all they had wanted to do was send him to his death.

And *what* a death ...

The whole mountain shook as if it, too, shivered. Rocks fell down onto Bima's head in a shower, but he stood still, staring at the two shadows coming towards him, hardly daring to believe his eyes. Hardly daring to believe who these monsters must be.

For now he knew who they were. He had heard terrible stories of travellers in the mountains who had come face to face with two monsters who lived in a cave just like this one.

But he had never, ever, heard a story of anyone who had escaped.

Chapter 4
Two Terrible Giants

Bima lifted his club up high and stood, feet apart, at the mouth of the cave, ready for battle.

The thundering noise had stopped, and there was an eerie silence. Then, out of the blackness, came a low, rasping voice.

"Who is pulling up *our* trees and moving *our* rocks?" it said.

"Who is pulling up *our* trees and moving *our* rocks?" a second voice repeated. It was higher, and louder, and even more sinister than the first.

"Who dares destroy the home of Rukmaka?" the first voice hissed.

"Who dares destroy the home of Rukmakala?" the second voice said.

Bima stepped a little closer. "It is I, Bima," he said bravely. "And I have no wish to destroy anything. I only want to find the Water of Life."

"There is no Water of Life here!" both voices roared. "And now – death to he who destroys our home!"

And with that, out stepped the two terrible giants, Rukmaka and Rukmakala. They stood high above Bima, and glared down at him. Then they picked up sharp rocks and hurled them at him. Their aim was good and soon Bima was badly injured.

Bima stood still with blood streaming down his face. Soon the giants grew tired of throwing rocks. They strode down and stared at him. Their red eyes bulged out in wonder. Never before had anyone stood up to them like this.

Still Bima stood, like a noble tree, hiding every trace of fear. Never before had *he* seen (or smelt) such horrible brutes!

Rukmaka and his brother Rukmakala were bigger and stronger than Bima. Rukmaka's skin was pink and Rukmakala's was blue, but both had long, wild, golden hair that stood out like a tangled mane. Their fat bellies shone with sweat. Their mouths hung open to show rows of glittering fangs.

And the more they looked at Bima, the more they drooled, and licked their lips.

"What have we here, brother Rukmakala?" whispered Rukmaka. "A tasty meal, if ever there was one!"

"What have we here, brother Rukmaka?" echoed Rukmakala. "Enough flesh for us both!"

And then, in the same moment, they jumped on Bima. They grabbed his arms, sniffed them carefully all along their length, then sank their teeth in and crunched, right to the bone.

For a moment, the pain was so terrible that Bima could neither think nor move. Then, with a roar, he shook his arms so hard that Rukmakala fell off and rolled down the mountain. Rukmaka however, still held on to Bima with his jaws.

But now Bima's club-hand was free. Blow after blow he beat down onto Rukmaka's

head, till at last the giant let go and fell at his feet.

Quick as an arrow, Bima picked Rukmaka up by the hair, and spun him round and round his head, faster and faster, like a whirl-wind. And as he spun, clouds of earth and stone were sucked up into the sky, till the mountain grew dark as night.

Still Bima spun the giant round his head, and then, when it seemed that the very mountains would be swept away, he let go.

As Rukmaka flew through the air, his cries of pain and rage rolled down the mountain and terrified the birds and animals from far and wide. Then, with one huge crash, he hit the side of the cave and landed, lifeless, on the rocky ground.

But Bima's ordeal was not over. One giant was dead, but the other was clawing its way back to fight again. Purple with rage, Rukmakala came lumbering towards him.

"Kill my brother, would you?" he roared, leaping into the air and kicking Bima hard in the belly.

"Well, Bima the great hero, you will *not* kill me!" And Rukmakala gave Bima such a mighty blow that he bent over with pain.

Then the Battle of the Giants really began. Again and again, Rukmakala tore Bima's club from his hand and dashed it to the ground. Again and again, he hit Bima with bone-splitting blows that made him howl in agony.

Again and again, Bima held back his cries, hid his fear, and fought for his life.

Time stood still. No one knows how long
Bima struggled, or understands the pain he
felt. But at last, hardly able to breathe, he
summoned his last drop of strength, and,
with one last, desperate lunge, he grabbed
his club. He swung it so hard at Rukmakala's
head that the giant's huge skull broke. With a
thud the giant fell to the ground.

Bima gazed down at Rukmakala. He could hardly believe that he had won the fight. Did the vast blue belly still move? Was there life left in the giant?

But there was none. The giant lay dead at his feet.

Bima sank to the ground. He was sore all over, and his brow boiled.

I shall rest for a while, he thought. *Then, I shall slice the heads off those two giants, for they are even greater prizes than the ogre's head!*

As Bima rested, the clouds of dust in the sky cleared, and the sun shone again. Bima let its warmth soothe his tired bones.

But why, he thought suddenly, did the sun's heat not burn him?

Why did his head, which had been on fire, feel cooler than ever? Where had the fresh breeze come from?

Bima stood up and looked round. Everything was as before. The dark mouth of the cave yawned above him, and the dead bodies of the giants lay twisted among the rocks.

Then, a most wonderful thing happened. As Bima walked towards the giants' bodies, they began to vanish before his very eyes! And at the same time, on the breath of the cooling breeze, came words he had not heard for a long, long time. Words that made his heart swell with joy.

"Bima," that breeze whispered lovingly in his ear. "Bima, my dear son!"

Chapter 5
The Water of Life

"Father!" cried Bima, running towards the two noble figures that stood where the giants' dead bodies had been. "Can it really be you?"

Vayu, the Wind God, smiled. He placed his hands, with their long magic thumb-nails, on Bima's shoulders. At once, Bima felt calm and safe. He gazed in wonder at his father and his friend, who he knew to be Indra, the Sky God.

He was bursting to find out why the two gods had been changed into giants, but he knew better than to ask. One day, perhaps, Vayu would tell him the story. But not now!

"We both must thank you for rescuing us from our prisons," Vayu said. "We could only escape if someone killed Rukmaka and Rukmakala, and, until now, there was no hero brave enough!"

Vayu went on, "And now you must return to Durna at once." He looked at Indra. "This time," he said, smiling, "Durna will give you the right directions to the Water of Life, believe me!"

And, with a great gust of wind and a sparkling of stars, Vayu the Wind God and Indra the Sky God were gone.

Bima set off at once. He was back at the palace in the twinkling of an arrow-head. And this time, he was glad to see that his old teacher was alone.

Durna hobbled towards him. "Our hero has returned!" he said, taking the ogre's head with his twisted hand. "Well done, Bima!"

Bima, however, was in no mood for praise. "You and Suyudana tricked me, and almost led me to my death," he said.

"Now, tell me truly where I can find the Water of Life," he went on sternly. "For my wish for Ever-lasting Happiness is stronger than ever."

Durna smiled. He stroked his curly beard.

"You will find the Water of Life in a world filled with light, and no shadows," he said.

A world filled with light, and no shadows? Bima thought. *Where on earth could that be?*

Then he understood what Durna meant. The Water of Life was to be found at the bottom of the sea!

Once more, he listened to Durna's directions. This time, Bima felt sure he could trust his teacher. Now he knew that Suyudana was the evil one.

He hurried home, where his mother was waiting for him.

"I am happy to see you safe, Bima," his mother said, as she hugged him close, "for I have been very worried about you."

Then Bima told his mother of his new plans to find the Water of Life. She was not at all pleased!

"So Durna has talked you into setting off on another quest," she said, looking up at him with a sad smile. "My dear son – why do you trust a man who has tried to kill you?"

Bima listened to his mother's words but, as always, he was set on doing what he thought was right. Turning his back on her, he marched off over mountains and valleys, forests and deserts, till he came to the sea. He stood on the sand and gazed out over the waves.

The Water of Life was at the bottom of this sea, he knew. But how was he to get there?

As he stood watching the waves, he saw a strange rippling in the distant water. It looked as if something was swimming just below the surface.

Swimming straight for him.

"Can it be a huge fish?" thought Bima. But this dark shape cut through the water like a spear. It was too long and pointed to be a fish.

Still Bima stared, frozen to the spot, as the waves parted before his eyes. Nearer and nearer the dark shape came, but still he could not see what it was. Then, before he had time to turn and run, the waters frothed and boiled. Out of the steaming water soared a great blue-green sea serpent.

If Bima had fought for his life with the giant Rukmaka, he fought even harder with the sea serpent. Its massive body wound round and round him, pinning his arms to his sides. It bit him, and its deadly poison filled his body. He could not move.

What good was his club now? What good were his magic thumb-nails?

As the sea serpent squeezed Bima ever tighter, the sky grew dark and flames leapt from the depths of the sea. Tidal waves swept over the land.

Lightning struck and thunder boomed. Everywhere – in every corner of the earth – there was noise and chaos.

And then, in one flash of deep red poison, it was over. The waves were calm. The earth was silent.

Bima, the hero, was dead.

He had failed in his quest to find Ever-lasting Happiness for himself and everyone he loved. Rain wept from the sky, and no bird sang.

Then, from the heavens, Tunggal, the greatest god of all, spoke.

"Wake up, Bima," he said, and Bima's huge body began to stir. Slowly, and painfully, he rose to his feet, shading his eyes against the great light that was the god, Tunggal.

"You have been brave," Tunggal went on. "And you have trusted those who were not as honest as you. Come ..."

Bima turned round and saw that the sea had vanished. All he could see was Tunggal, with golden light all round him. And Tunggal was calling to him.

"Come, Bima," he said with a smile. "You have learnt much on your quests. You have learnt how cruel the world can be, and how good can over-come evil. Now you will have your reward ..."

Bima did not know where Tunggal was leading him. Yet he put his trust in him and kept on walking. The golden light blinded him, yet he went on walking till at last he was right inside Tunggal. It was like being in Heaven.

And there, bathed in the god's light, was a shrine with five levels.

On the top level was a golden casket.

"The Water of Life is inside the casket," Bima heard Tunggal telling him. "Take it, and use it wisely."

Bima thanked Tunggal. Then, with great pride, he carried the casket, with the Water of Life inside it, home.

****

In the coming years there were many more quests that were full of danger for Bima, and there were many bitter battles for him to fight. He often risked his life, but you can be sure he always fought for what he thought was right, like the brave hero he was.

And you can be sure that he tried his very best, always, to bring happiness to the people he loved.

BATTLE CARDS

Franzeska G. Ewart

Author

Favourite hero:
A pigeon called White Vision who saved 11 members of crew during World War Two. It couldn't see because of the fog yet it flew 60 miles over rough seas to raise the alarm.

Favourite monster:
Ravana, an Indian monster-god with 10 heads.

Your weapon of choice:
A cloak of invisibility.

Favourite fight scene:
David and Goliath. David was just a boy and Goliath was a huge giant of a man, yet David had the courage to face him with only a catapult.

Goodie or baddie:
Goodie.

RELOADED

WHO WILL WIN?

Sandeep Kaushik

Illustrator

Favourite hero:
Goku – the main character in the Dragon Ball manga and anime series.

Favourite monster:
Frieza – a supervillain, also from Dragon Ball. He rules over 79 planets! He can take five different forms, one of which has horns, a spiked tail and talon-like toes!

Your weapon of choice:
A sword.

Your special secret power:
Super speed.

Goodie or baddie:
Goodie.

RELOADED

Barrington Stoke would like to thank all its readers for commenting on the manuscript before publication and in particular:

Theo Gerrard Anderson

Amy Harper

Sue Black

George Hooley

David Britteon

George Hopson

Oliver Burrows

S. Leszczynsk

Liam Carney

Ben McCarthy

Mark Frith

Jacob Pothecary

Harry Fisher

James Simpson

Jenny Gooch

Linda Tobert

Become a Consultant!

Would you like to give us feedback on our titles before they are published? Contact us at the email address below – we'd love to hear from you!

info@barringtonstoke.co.uk
www.barringtonstoke.co.uk